I0623245

DEBRA CASTANEDA

THE HAUNTING OF CHAVEZ RAVINE

SHADOW
CANYON
— press —

ISBN: 979-8-9903956-2-6
Edited by: Lyndsey Smith, Horrorsmith Editing
Cover design by: James, GoOnWrite.com

To Rachel
for sharing her memories of Chavez Ravine

Chapter 1

Lily Bantacorte made dinner and said a little prayer to El Santo Nino de Atocha for help. Not that she'd given him any reason to intercede on her behalf. She couldn't remember the last time she'd gone to church. And even if the holy child, with his serene, gentle expression, decided to take pity on her, how could he hear her plea over all the commotion in the kitchen?

The three-bedroom house in Boyle Heights had seemed big enough just the year before, but it appeared to have shrunk after her mother's wedding at La Purisima Church.

Callate—please, be quiet.

There was never a moment of peace with two brothers and now a stepfather, who had wandering hands when no one was looking.

Lily knew she should tell her mother about Emiliano, but she couldn't bring herself to do it. Her mother was so in love with him and believed all his lies, even though everyone else could see he was a no-good womanizer.

And so, with her mother working late into the evening, cleaning offices, Lily was left to take care of her brothers and Emiliano, or as she referred to him, the cochino—the nasty man.

Emiliano came into the kitchen and pressed against her back, reaching past her to snatch a tortilla. Lily sidestepped away, pretending it hadn't happened.

Just like she always did.

The cochino unnerved her. He was a towering figure with muscular arms and piercing dark eyes. Some women gushed over his good looks, but they didn't know him like she did—didn't see the cold smile hidden beneath his mustache. Lily sometimes felt like she was trapped in a cage with a jaguar.

Emiliano pouted and threw himself into a chair, like a child denied a treat.

Lily fought the urge to whack him on the head with her library book, *Tomorrow Will Be Better*, which was still sitting untouched on a shelf. In this household, there was never any time for reading, no moment to relax after a long day of work.

Although sparsely furnished, the Bantacortes had one of the nicer houses in the neighborhood, with a good-sized living room and a wide front porch. After finishing his shift at the railyard, Emiliano could have chosen to relax on the wooden swing outside. Instead, he sat in the kitchen, squeezed between the big white stove and the Hoosier cabinet dwarfing the room.

You don't have to stay, the little voice in Lily's head said.

But where would she go? She'd tried to find a roommate but hadn't had any luck. The girls at work either lived at home, helping to support their families, or they were already married. And Lily couldn't afford an apartment on her own.

She shut her eyes and stirred the pot of beef stew she'd made over the weekend. Emiliano and the boys wanted taquitos too. They were always hungry and noisy and demanding.

The screen door banged open, and her brothers stomped in.

When Frankie saw Lily hadn't yet started frying the taquitos, he shrieked, "We're hungry!"

She gazed down at them, tenderness fighting with exasperation. Both had heart-shaped faces, like hers, with enormous dark eyes fringed with black lashes. Suspenders held up their pants—hand-me-downs from the big brother they couldn't remember. The Bantacortes weren't poor, but nothing ever went to waste.

Lily ruffled his hair. "Ay, Frankie! What's wrong with you?"

Frankie fell to the floor, clutching his stomach. "I'm starving, that's what. All the other kids ate already."

Beto joined the dramatics, raising a hand to his forehead. "I'm so hungry, I'm going to faint."

From behind them, Emiliano strummed his guitar. "Your sister is a big shot now, muchachos. She doesn't care about us anymore. We're nobodies. Just mouths to feed."

That got the boys' attention.

They looked up, eyes wide, stomachs temporarily forgotten.

Beto's pupils glittered with suspicion. "What does he mean?"

Frankie, the youngest, seemed about to cry.

Emiliano coughed loudly, but Lily refused to give him the satisfaction of acknowledging whatever he was about to say.

"Your mom says Liliana got a big promotion at work. She's not sewing anymore. She's doing paperwork or something for the big boss at the factory. But what I want to know is…how she got that job. Because they don't give those jobs to Mexican girls. Unless she's been up to no good with her boss. I wouldn't put it past her. So now, she doesn't care if she lets us starve."

Her stepfather's eyes burned a hole in the back of her head.

That wasn't the first time Lily had been subjected to such vile remarks. One night, he'd cornered her on the porch and accused her of all sorts of disgusting things.

The truth was, she'd been lucky to get the job. The previous clerk had fallen ill and never returned. On a sweltering morning at the factory, Lily noticed the boss struggling with paperwork and had offered to help. He was surprised by her ability to type, a skill she had taught herself, and her proficiency in English. It was easier for him to promote her than find someone new. Plus, Lily could translate for the Spanish-speaking workers.

Frankie and Beto stared up at her like she had betrayed them. They were too young to understand. It wasn't their fault their stepfather was so mean, but she couldn't find it within herself to feel much of anything besides annoyance.

Lily waved an impatient hand at them. "Ay, I'll never get dinner done with you two pestering me. Go outside and play."

They trudged toward the door, heads hanging, arms at their sides.

She called after them. "Stay out of the alley and make sure you can hear me when I call you."

On the porch, Frankie wailed, "But the other kids are in the alley."

Before Emiliano came to live with them, Lily's brothers had treated her with the same respect they showed their mother. But once they saw how Emiliano behaved, they began to mimic his insolent ways. Lily didn't know how much more she could take.

She crossed to the screen door, flung it open, and stood on the threshold, hands on her hips. The words were out of her mouth before she could stop them. "I don't care what the other kids are doing. Don't you dare go into the alley. If you do, do you know what's going to happen to you? The Llorona is going to get you!"

Frankie screamed. Beto stumbled backward, tripping over a metal bucket.

Frankie wrapped his arms around Beto's waist, burying his face into his brother's side. Beto put an arm around Frankie's bony shoulders.

"Don't listen to her, Frankie. She's just being mean." Beto glared at Lily. "Tell him you didn't mean it."

The ground seemed to shift beneath Lily's feet. "I didn't mean it, Frankie. She's not real."

"You're lying," Frankie cried. "She *is* real. She killed Tomas, and you know it."

They hadn't talked about what happened to Tomas for a long time. La Llorona was a forbidden subject in their home, and even saying her name made Lily's mouth feel like it was filled with dirty water and death.

"I'm sorry." Lily's voice was heavy with remorse. "I shouldn't have said that. You boys go play, but please, stay in the yard, okay?"

Beto surprised her by nodding and guiding Frankie toward the overgrown area on the side of the house, where they could pretend they were lost in a jungle.

Emiliano leaned back in his chair, hands coming up behind his head, a smirk on his face. "Your mom told me about Tomas. That you were lollygagging and let La Llorona take him at Echo Park Lake."

The words hit like a slap to the face.

Lily's mother had always blamed herself for what happened that day. She said she should never have left the rambunctious Tomas and his cousins with young Lily. They had proven to be too much for her to handle alone.

But maybe that wasn't true. Maybe her mother really did blame her. Why else would Emiliano say such a thing?

Lily ignored him and turned her back on the man, which was never a good idea, but she needed to finish making dinner. She spread mashed potatoes onto a corn tortilla, hands shaking.

In that moment, El Santo Nino must have taken pity on her. Suddenly, she had the answer to her problems.

Lencha.

Lily hadn't thought of her Aunt Lencha in years. Her father's only sister lived in Chavez Ravine, and at her father's funeral, Lencha had invited Lily to live with her and learn the practice of healing.

At the time, Lily had just started a new job at the garment factory, so she'd politely turned down the offer.

Lencha hadn't seemed the least bit offended. "If you ever change your mind, you know where to find me."

Which wasn't true.

Lily had never visited Lencha's house, but she was sure she could find it. Her aunt lived alone somewhere in the hills above Chinatown.

With her mind made up, Lily lowered the taquitos into the bubbling oil. After dinner, she cleaned up, locked herself in her bedroom, and packed a suitcase.

Chapter 2

The next day after work, instead of heading home, Lily made her way to Broadway and hopped onto a streetcar. She got off at the bottom of Bishop Road with a handful of other passengers. From there, they all walked up a steep dirt track leading to Chavez Ravine and La Loma, the neighborhood where her aunt lived.

She at least remembered that much.

Lily had heard some people who lived in Chavez Ravine hardly ever left their neighborhoods, and now she understood why. The journey wasn't an easy one, especially when carrying something heavy, like she was. Lily followed a man in a derby hat up the hill, her cardboard suitcase growing heavier with each step.

The day began to slip away, the October sun's warm glow giving way to a chilly autumn evening. Lily didn't want to stop and retrieve the sweater from her suitcase. Instead, she walked faster, determined not to lose sight of the man just ahead of her.

It was a lonely place, with Elysian Park looming in the distance. The tops of the trees gave the impression of hunchbacked creatures, and she didn't want to be alone on the path.

The uphill walk gave her time with her thoughts.

Lily's mother had burst into tears when she announced she was leaving. She begged and pleaded for Lily to stay, but she had stood firm.

Her mother's face had turned bright red. "How can you be so selfish, Liliana? Who's going to help me watch after your brothers?"

Lily thought that was unfair. If she'd been married, with children of her own, her mother wouldn't expect her to babysit. Emiliano didn't have any kids. He lived in their house and contributed little to its upkeep, so he could keep an eye on Beto and Frankie. After all, he *was* their stepfather.

"Aunt Carmen lives just around the block," Lily had said stiffly. "The boys can stay with her until you get home."

Lily and her mother rarely argued, and their exchange weighed heavily on her heart.

The man in the hat disappeared around an enormous nopales cactus.

And what if her aunt didn't welcome her? Lencha could sometimes be dour, a spinster of few words. For all Lily knew, Lencha would scold her for abandoning her mother and send her straight home.

A glimmer in the sky caught Lily's attention—a burst of crimson light winking from the north. It danced along the tops of the trees, growing in size before tumbling down a desolate, parched hill and vanishing.

It happened so fast, Lily thought she must have imagined it. She paused, scanning the slope for the strange red light. Where had it gone?

A chilling sense of foreboding settled in the pit of her stomach.

Lily hurried to the top of the hill. She made her way past a tricycle, a broken fence, and a dilapidated wooden shed, carefully avoiding the spines sticking out of the cactus paddles.

A cluster of people gathered in the middle of the dusty road. A few others were scattered behind flimsy fences or perched on the front porches of their white clapboard houses. They talked excitedly, and Lily wondered if they had seen the red light too.

The man with the hat was there, clutching his lunch pail and frowning. "Oh, come on now, Sal," he said. "Don't mess around like that."

Sal was a burly man, the muscles bulging under his dirty work shirt suggesting a day spent doing manual labor. "I'm not messing around. I told you, I saw her. She was flying over the trees at Elysian Park. It was La Llorona."

A woman with short, curly brown hair clutched his arm. "I saw her too. I was hanging the clothes, and then she was right here in my yard. She *spoke* to me."

Sal's eyebrows shot up. "That's the first I've heard of La Llorona talking. Doesn't she just kill people?"

The woman shoved her hands into the pockets of her apron, an expression on her face like a storm cloud about to burst. "I heard her, and there's nothing wrong with my ears. She talked loud and clear."

Sal scratched the side of his face. "And what did she tell you, Betty?"

All eyes in the small group shifted to Betty, who cleared her throat before speaking. "She said 'Cuidado,' but in a real ugly way. Like, she growled it."

Lily's eyes widened in astonishment. Whatever she'd been expecting the woman to say, it wasn't that. The weeping woman was known to scream and sob, but Lily had never heard of her speaking. Certainly never cautioning people.

"Betty's no mentirosa," said a tiny old lady wearing a faded pink mandil over a long gray dress. "I saw the Llorona in her yard too. I've lived here for a long time, and I've never seen her here before."

Sal jerked his head in Lily's direction. "Maybe she brought her."

Lily felt dizzy. The man couldn't possibly know about what had happened with Tomas and La Llorona. Dread unspooled like heavy coils in her chest, and her suitcase felt like it carried the weight of that terrible day at Echo Park Lake.

Her brother's face, drained of color and twisted in terror...

His horrified expression had told Lily he hadn't just drowned. Something unimaginable had happened to Tomas. His cousins swore they'd seen the ghostly figure of La Llorona, heard her let out an unearthly wail.

Others at the park had sworn they saw her too—a few construction workers on their lunch break, several passers-by. Which was why Lily knew she was not to blame.

Because once La Llorona set her sights on someone, they were doomed.

The man holding the lunch pail said, "Are you lost?"

Lily cleared her throat. "I'm looking for Lencha Bantacorte's house." When no one answered, she added, "She's my aunt."

Betty and the old woman exchanged glances, but it was Sal who said, "You don't know where your tia lives?" His voice was full of disapproval.

A surge of defensiveness rose within Lily, but she pushed it down. There was no use getting off on the wrong foot. Her father had lived in the ravine before moving to Boyle Heights, and he always said everyone knew everybody's business.

"It's been a while since I've seen her," she admitted.

The elderly woman tilted her head and studied Lily with narrowed eyes. "You know a thing or two about La Llorona, if I remember right."

That got everyone's attention. They raised their eyebrows in surprise.

"How's that?" Sal asked, staring straight at Lily.

When she didn't answer, the old woman did. "It's a sad story about this young lady's little brother. Lencha's nephew. You know how La Llorona haunts the lake at Echo Park? Well, the little boy got too close to the water, poracito, and she pulled him in."

Betty gasped and crossed herself.

"Is it true?" The man with the lunchbox sounded skeptical.

Lily sighed. There was no use lying.

"I didn't see La Llorona myself." It was a vague answer, and it clearly disappointed her small audience. "Can someone tell me where Lencha lives?"

Sal marched up the street, gesturing over his shoulder. "I'll show you."

Lily snatched her suitcase and hurried after him.

"Watch out for *La Llorona*," Betty called.

No one laughed.

When Lily turned to wave goodbye, the old lady crossed herself.

Lily followed Sal to the top of the street, which dipped down into a ravine dotted with houses. Her companion had deep crinkles around his eyes and skin browned by the sun, but he was younger than she had first thought. Somewhere in his early thirties.

Beyond the crisscross of streets, a dirt road with houses on either side rose into the hills toward the edge of Elysian Park. Lily's heart fell. She hoped Lencha didn't live all the way up there.

Sal pointed. "Go down this street until you see a water tank. Keep on going 'til you get to a bunch of mailboxes and make a left. Lencha's house is the one with the big palm tree on the side. It's a good thing you came before it gets dark. There's only one streetlight in La Loma."

Lily thanked him and hurried down the road. The dusty, desolate slopes reached up on either side of the unpaved street. To her left was a ravine choked with small trees and brush. Somewhere, Mexican music blared from a radio. Several young children chasing after a goat suddenly appeared in front of her before turning into a nearby alleyway.

There were no sidewalks. The houses varied in size and condition—some were small and rundown, with overgrown yards and shaky wooden fences; others looked like her own in Boyle Heights, clapboards painted white, peaked roofs and welcoming porches. A few even had a second floor.

Lily's shoes pinched her feet, and her toes throbbed.

Lencha's house was smaller than all the others on the block, the wood unpainted and faded by the sun. An overhang sagged over the narrow porch, and a jelly palm tree hugged the far side of the house. A narrow alley separated Lencha's house from its humble neighbor.

Something bumped her leg, and Lily jumped.

It was just a small goat.

After a few half-hearted bleats, its head nudged her knee, and it ambled away, disappearing behind a shed.

Two men, bent over a car engine, paused their tinkering and stared.

Lily quickly stepped toward the front door.

There was no need to knock. The door was open. Her aunt's stern expression met her gaze.

"Tia," Lily said.

Lencha pulled her inside. "I was wondering when you'd get here."

Her aunt wasn't the kissing or hugging type. Instead, Lily received an awkward pat on the arm.

Lily set down her suitcase and wriggled her sore fingers. "How did you know I was coming?"

Lencha tapped the side of her head. "I know things." She paused. "What I don't know is why you're here, but I can guess. Does it have something to do with that stepfather of yours?"

Lily had to clear her throat before she could get the words out. "He and the boys got to be a little too much for me. I feel bad, leaving my poor mom. She—"

Lencha held up a hand, frown deepening.

"She's a grown woman, Liliana, and you have your own life to live. Your dad and I didn't always see eye to eye, but if he were still alive, he'd agree with me. I knew Emiliano was up to no good. He was at the funeral, remember? Already sniffing around, with one eye on you. When I heard your mom was going to marry the fool, I knew it was just a matter of time before he started acting up."

Lily was speechless.

Lencha continued. "I'm glad you came. You can stay as long as you want. You still got that same job?"

Lily nodded. "I got a promotion. I can pay rent."

"Ay, no!" Lencha sounded scandalized. "But you can help me with my cures. I'll show you what to do."

Lily didn't know the first thing about curanderia, just that Lencha had learned it growing up on a ranch in Mexico. "I'm happy to help you, but I'm not sure I'll be very good at it."

"You're smart," Lencha said brusquely. "You can learn what I have to teach you."

Despite her aunt's stern demeanor, Lily felt comfortable around her. She glanced around the small living room. The furnishings were sparse, but the sofa and small table fit the space perfectly.

Lily's gaze moved to the open door, and she was surprised to discover twilight had arrived. The indigo sky was streaked with shades of violet.

Lencha stood silently, staring outside, mouth opening slightly. She gradually made her way toward the front door as if in a trance.

Gooseflesh rose on Lily's arms. "Are you all right, Tia?"

Lencha pushed open the old, creaky screen door and stepped out onto the porch, her long black braid trailing down her back.

She gripped a post, leaned forward, and peered in both directions, then stepped out onto the road. Lencha slowly scanned the rooftops of the neighboring houses.

Lily watched her aunt with growing alarm.

Suddenly, Lencha spoke. "She's here."

Fear skittered up Lily's arms like tiny spiders.

A mournful wail pierced the quiet, echoing through the ravine. Down the street, a door banged open. The cry of anguish intensified.

People ran out of their houses, eyes searching the treetops. When they spotted Lencha, they gathered behind her, as if she could protect them from the terrible noise.

No one had to tell Lily what had made the horrible sound—the answer was written all over the panicked expressions of the neighbors.

It was the cry of La Llorona.

Chapter 3

Lily awoke with a start, shivering and alone on the small bed. She'd cowered through the long night, while La Llorona's wails assaulted them from high up in the dark hills.

As bad as the sound was, the silence was almost worse. Lily's entire body would tense, ears straining to hear the haunting cries.

Lencha had paced in front of the windows, barely sleeping. Before the frightened neighbors returned to their homes, she had advised them to burn a handful of chiles pasillas to ward off the wandering spirit, and she had done the same. The house was redolent with the pungent smoke.

Lily's eyes had watered, and she had fits of coughing, but she didn't complain. Not if burned chiles kept the phantom from their door.

La Llorona had finally stopped her crying just after two o'clock in the morning.

A quick glance at her wristwatch told Lily it was just past six o'clock. She let out a tired yawn, already feeling drained, even though the day had only begun. Her boss wouldn't care about the noisy ghost keeping her up all night.

Lily took a quick bath and dressed in the tiny bedroom. When she walked past Lencha's room, she saw no sign of her aunt. The bed was neatly made. Maybe Lencha hadn't slept at all.

In the kitchen, a pot of beans simmered on the stove, and there was fresh coffee too—strong and delicious, flavored with a cinnamon stick and sweetened with piloncillo.

Their encounter with La Llorona had left Lily feeling shaky.

Voices sounded from the backyard, but before going outside to investigate, she wanted to enjoy a few moments of solitude in the quiet kitchen. At home, she'd had to wake up early and get her brothers ready for school before rushing off to catch the bus to work. Enjoying a morning coffee in peace was a new experience.

Lily settled into her seat at the kitchen table and took in her new surroundings. The small room was tidy and cozy, with a wooden counter along one wall. It was covered in clay plates and pear-shaped jugs. Half-burned candles sat in shallow bowls. Dried herbs bound with strings hung from nails in the wall over a molcajete.

This must be where Lencha makes her cures.

According to Lily's mother, the kitchen was where the trouble started between Raul and Lencha when they first came to the U.S. Raul wanted his sister to find a regular job and stop messing up their kitchen with her "damn hechizos," but Lencha had refused.

Lencha had quickly gained a reputation for her ability to heal just about any ailment that came her way in La Loma, and she earned more money than Raul Bantacorte as a result. When he wouldn't stop complaining, she told him to leave if he didn't like it. He *had* left, but he'd never forgiven his sister.

Lily could still remember the tension crackling in the air the few times her father and aunt had been in the same room: at church for her brother's baptisms, and a few nights of tamale making around Christmas.

She sipped her coffee while the voices in the backyard grew louder. A tap at the window broke her reverie. When Lily looked up, a woman's face in the window made her shriek.

The woman jumped back with a yelp. "Ay, it's just me—Betty. We met yesterday, remember?" she scolded through a gap in the window.

Heart still pounding, Lily got up and stepped closer. "Did you hear La Llorona too?"

Betty made a clucking noise. "You better believe it. We were too darned scared to leave our houses after she started up all that commotion."

Lily set the cup down in the sink. "My aunt isn't here."

More clucking. "Of course, she is. She's right where she's supposed to be. Working."

Lily was confused. Lencha hadn't mentioned anything about going to a job.

A moment later, Betty opened the side door and motioned Lily outside. The woman wore a belted floral dress and such a determined expression, Lily knew she had no choice but to follow, still wearing slippers on her feet.

The narrow passage between the houses led to a backyard much larger than Lily would have suspected. The space was a wild profusion of plants and herbs. A crooked wooden shed with a tin roof covered in vines squatted at the far end, and people were lined up outside of it, talking nervously about La Llorona.

More people emerged from a gap between an overgrown bush and a wide nopales cactus and joined the line.

Lily watched the hubbub, mystified. "What's going on?"

"They've come to see Lencha, that's what," Betty replied tartly. "They want her to protect them against La Llorona. She's never been seen around here before, and that's got everyone worried."

"Lencha's in the shed?"

"That's where she does her work. Or most of it, at least. Some of it she does in her kitchen, but she can't have the whole neighborhood tromping through her house."

Lily nodded absently. Betty took her elbow, guided her past the line of people, and pushed her way into the shed. Lencha was attending to a small boy and his mother. There was just enough room for the three of them, so Lily and Betty barely fit.

The room was chilly in the morning air, and everyone was bundled up. The mother sat in a low chair, the little boy of about six on her lap, coughing with watery eyes. Something was burning in a clay bowl. Lencha waved her hand over the smoke and guided it toward the boy, who scrunched up his face and turned away.

Lily stood next to her aunt, giving the boy an encouraging smile. He buried his head in his mother's bosom.

"What are you doing, Tia?"

"This little troublemaker here is having a problem with his throat. So I'm burning some of the fuzzy roots from a feather plant." Lencha placed two brown hands on the boy's shoulders. "But he's got to sniff it in if it's going to work. Right, mijo? And this stuff works to keep La Llorona away too, so if you don't want her showing up at the end of your bed tonight, mister, take a few big sniffs."

Lily thought that was going a bit far, but it worked. The boy sat up and regarded Lencha with a wary expression.

His mother kissed him on the top of his head. "You heard Senora Bantacorte, mijo."

The child pouted but complied. Lily watched him inhale the smoke, body quivering.

After Lencha was satisfied he'd had enough, the mother handed Lencha a sack of flour and left. Lily's aunt added it to a pile of other items resting on a small table, then poured water from a jug and rinsed her hands. She grabbed a paper bag and gave it to Lily.

Lily opened it. Several pieces of pan dulce were nestled inside. Her stomach grumbled.

"People always find a way to pay," Betty said to Lily, then turned to Lencha. "You've been busy this morning."

"Ay, yes." Lencha looked past her, at the line outside the door. "It's a bad time for Catalina to be away. Her cousin is expecting a baby any day now, so who knows how long she'll be gone."

Betty shook her head. "So it's just you, then."

"Who's Catalina?" Lily asked.

Lencha plucked a small whisk broom from its hook and swept the surface of her worktable, scattering dried herbs to the ground. "Another curandera. She lives in Palo Verde, so when she's gone, people come see me."

Betty snorted. "I don't know why you two ladies lie like you do. You're brujas, and everybody knows it."

"We are what people need us to be." Lencha sighed. "And you should know *why* we don't go around calling ourselves brujas. Remember when that pendejo down the street thought I put a hechizo on him so he'd stop beating his wife? He showed up drunk, with a knife."

Lily gasped. "That's terrible."

"That's not the half of it," Lencha said dryly.

Betty gave Lencha's arm a pat. "You're right. I'm sorry. I forgot about that. At least you have your niece to help you now."

Lily cleared her throat. "I'm not sure I'll be much help, but I can try."

The two older women gazed at her, clearly disappointed by her hesitation. Or maybe it was her lack of enthusiasm. Or both.

Lily mustered a smile. "Maybe you can show me what to do when I come back from work?"

She nervously smoothed the front of her skirt, noticing a loose thread dangling from the hem. Lily spotted a pair of scissors hanging from a hook and grabbed them, snipping off the offending string.

Lencha let out a sharp gasp.

"Ay, no! Those are my *special* scissors. I only use them for my work. No one else can use them." She noticed Lily's startled expression and gently took the scissors from her hand. Lencha carefully placed them back on the hook with a heavy sigh. "It's all right. You didn't know. But you'll need to have your own scissors, and you need to pick them out yourself. Can you buy some when you're in town? Just make sure they're made of iron and they feel comfortable in your hand."

By "her work," Lencha meant medicine and magic.

The idea of entering the mysterious realm of brujeria both intrigued and frightened Lily. She'd grown up listening to hushed whispers about her aunt. Now, faced with traditions she knew nothing about, she was filled with trepidation.

But she had no choice. Lencha might refuse rent, but it was clear she expected Lily to contribute in other ways, especially after the arrival of La Llorona.

Still, nothing would drive her back home, where Emiliano lurked. Lily would do anything to avoid him and his hands.

"I'll make sure to get a good pair," she promised.

The older woman gave her a nod of approval before turning back to her workbench.

Lily emerged from the shed, eyes blinking in the bright morning light. She looked at the faces of the people waiting for Lencha's help—mothers and their children, a mix of hope and desperation in their eyes. Lily suddenly understood why Lencha had chosen curanderia over a regular job, why she preferred to work in her cramped shed rather than in a factory or an office.

If these people didn't have Lencha to listen to them and to help them, they would have no one at all.

Chapter 4

It was so busy at work, Lily didn't get a lunch break. The autumn sun beat down on the old factory. It felt like working in an oven. The ceiling fans just blew around the hot air, and by the time Lily clocked out, her skin was slick with sweat.

The oppressive heat followed her to Newberry's at the corner of 5th and Broadway. There, Lily tested several pairs of scissors, rejecting those that felt too flimsy and finally settling on a pair with red handles. She liked the heft of them in her hand—heavy enough to suggest they could be relied upon no matter what the task.

On the streetcar, she collapsed into a seat behind a harried mother with three young children. The hot day had left her so drained, Lily nodded off just minutes after settling in, the small paper bag holding the scissors on her lap.

Lily woke with a start, feeling someone staring at her. She glanced around the streetcar.

A shadowy figure sat across the aisle. It was blurry, as if shrouded in a sheer white veil, features pressed into the cloth. Although she couldn't see the eyes, Lily could feel its gaze, intense and unrelenting.

Despite the heat, she couldn't help but shiver. Lily clutched the paper bag against her chest and rubbed her eyes to clear away the sleep, but still, she couldn't see the figure clearly. Panic bloomed in her chest.

Lily looked around. The streetcar was packed with people, hot and sweaty and fanning themselves, but no one appeared to have noticed the mysterious figure sitting across from her.

Maybe she was overly tired and imagining things. Or maybe it was the heat. Lily gazed out the window, counted to twenty, and then looked back inside.

The figure was now standing in the aisle, inches away.

A smell hit Lily like a wave, a nauseating stench of filthy water and decaying flesh. She gagged, shrinking back into her seat. For one horrible moment, Lily expected the shroud-covered figure to slide into the vacant seat beside her, but instead, it glided away, stopping next to the woman and her children, none of whom seemed to notice.

The figure's face was still obscured by the shawl, but strands of damp, dark hair peeked out from the thin material.

La Llorona.

It *had* to be La Llorona. But why did no one else see her? What was she doing on the streetcar?

The ghostly figure bent over the little girl sitting closest to the aisle. Elongated fingers stretched out of the shroud and toward her small body.

A scream rose in Lily's throat, and her hands spasmed on the paper bag.

The scissors!

They were just ordinary scissors from the five and dime. Lencha hadn't explained how they were supposed to be used in brujeria, but Lily had to do something. She slipped them out of the bag and brandished them in the air.

That caught the specter's attention.

Its head swiveled toward her. A clawed, withered hand stopped just inches from the little girl's unsuspecting face.

Another foul blast made Lily's eyes water.

Not knowing what else to do, Lily gripped the scissors with both hands, quickly opening and closing them as if La Llorona were a bit of cloth she intended to cut.

The white-shrouded apparition shrunk back.

Encouraged, Lily stood on shaking legs and repeated the motion, praying it would be enough to drive away the ghost.

La Llorona let out a spine-chilling shriek, which made the other passengers turn and stare, confusion etched on their faces. They looked right through the phantom and straight at Lily.

There was terror in the children's eyes gazing up at her—a crazy lady holding a pair of scissors just above their heads.

The ghost faded into nothingness.

"You didn't see her?" Lily cried. "La Llorona. She was here!"

The passengers now looked around frantically. But soon enough, all eyes landed back on Lily, who still clutched the scissors like a weapon.

"I don't know what you're up to, lady." A man with leathery brown skin stood up and pointed at her. "But you better put those tijeras away. You're scaring people."

Lily quickly followed his advice. When the streetcar lurched to a stop, Lily snatched up her belongings and stumbled down the steps, eager to escape the staring, accusing eyes.

She found herself alone on a quiet corner not far from her mother's house, heart beating way too fast. Across the street, a man leaning against a lamppost stared. Lily was so rattled from her encounter with La Llorona, it took her a few moments to recognize him.

It was Emiliano, smoking a cigarette and wearing the brimmed hat he thought made him look like a movie star. When their eyes met, he tipped his hat, a threat somehow lurking behind the gesture.

Lily hurried inside a small market. She wandered the aisles, one eye on the door. Lily took her time, pretending to shop and hoping Emiliano would get bored and leave. When she finally pushed through the screen door of the market, he was gone.

Lily hurried toward La Loma, glancing over her shoulder for her stepfather, wondering how he'd happened to be there when she got off the streetcar. There was a newspaper stand nearby. Maybe he'd stopped to buy cigarettes. Nothing more than a coincidence.

Soon, her thoughts returned to La Llorona. How had she concealed her face? Why had she only revealed herself to Lily? And where had she gone?

Whatever the answers, the experience felt like a terrible omen.

Chapter 5

Lily waited until after dinner, when they were washing dishes, to tell her aunt about the appearance of La Llorona on the streetcar.

Lencha stared. "You've never seen her before?"

"No." Lily sighed. "Not even when my brother drowned at the lake. Other people said they saw her, but not me."

Lencha picked up a red-checked cloth and began drying the dishes. "Well, you're not the only one she's bothering. La Llorona was very busy around here while you were at work. There was a big commotion at the school in Palo Verde. The kids said they saw her on the playground.

"Ricky Torres, the iceman, came to see me. He said he was driving his delivery truck when he saw a woman at the bottom of the big hill in Bishop, and she was all covered up in white, even her head. He thought maybe she was a nun, so he stopped and asked if she wanted a ride. She got in but didn't talk. He kept trying to ask her questions, but she didn't say anything, and he couldn't see her face under the veil. And then he noticed a real bad smell, like old dirty water.

"When he looked over at her, it was like she was leaking, and the seat was all wet, and that's when he started to get scared. So he stopped the truck and told her to get out, but she didn't move, so he got out and went around to open the door and pull her out, but there was no one there."

The story made Lily shudder. "I know that smell."

"Ricky's brother drowned in a river in Mexico," Lencha continued. "He was just five. Everyone said La Llorona did it. Your brother drowned too, so I wonder if that's why she appeared the same way to both of you. To the school kids, she was a lady in a long black cloak, with a hood hiding her face.

"A bachelor in Palo Verde said a beautiful lady came to his door and started flirting with him. He was about to let her in, when he noticed she had feet like a goat, so he slammed the door. Then he heard something running back and forth on the roof of his house."

"Goat feet?" Lily gasped. "Do you think *that* was La Llorona?"

Lencha measured ground coffee into the jug. "She comes in many forms. It's like she can change anything she wants. What she looks like. What she wears. Where she appears. Sometimes, she cries and cries. Sometimes, she makes no sound at all. And don't get me started on what happened to her.

"There are a whole bunch of stories about that too. In some stories, she's lost her children, or they accidentally drowned. Other times, she's murdered them. Sometimes, she's full of sadness and remorse, and others, she's angry and vengeful, out to punish men because her lover wronged her."

Lencha poured hot water into the jug and set it on the table.

"Maybe she is who people want her to be."

Lily added milk and sugar to the cups Lencha set out. "But I don't want her to be *anything*. I don't want to see her at all. I want her to go away."

"What you want and what she wants are two different things," Lencha said wearily. "She's here for a reason. Whatever it is, I just hope she gives us a break tonight. We could all use a little rest."

Lencha turned her head and coughed. Lily didn't like the sound of it. It came from deep in her chest. She hoped Lencha wasn't getting sick.

Chapter 6

Just after midnight, Lily was roused from her sleep by the sound of her aunt's coughs coming through the thin wall separating their bedrooms. Lily lay there, wondering if she should get up and check on Lencha, but after a few minutes, all was quiet again. After a hot day, the weather had turned chilly, and she was grateful to stay in her warm bed.

Lily had just drifted off again when she startled awake. The faint sound of a woman crying was coming from the backyard.

Lily threw off the covers and swung her legs over the edge of the bed, muscles tensed. The sobs were haunting and full of despair.

She tiptoed to the window, the wooden floor feeling rough beneath her bare feet. Lily's heart pounded. She pulled back the curtains and peered outside.

Nothing other than the outlines of the wild garden and shadows cast by the moonlight.

The backyard looked much prettier at night, almost magical. Lily let out a shaky breath. There was no sign of La Llorona.

She turned back toward the bed, but a movement in the garden caught her eye. It was a figure floating above Lencha's shed, bathed in a strange glow.

Lily's breath caught in her throat.

It wasn't just her imagination. She had excellent eyesight and could clearly see a woman with long dark hair. The figure was luminous and slightly translucent.

An icy chill sped down Lily's spine.

Before she could even comprehend what she was seeing, the figure rushed toward her through the air, with the speed of a falcon diving for prey. A face pressed against the window glass, its features hideous and twisted, its open mouth a black, cavernous void. Lily gasped and stumbled backward.

And then the revolting figure was gone.

With her legs shaking, Lily flicked on the bedside lamp. She heard water running down the window and turned to see what was causing it. It was like someone outside was spraying the window with a hose. After what seemed like an eternity, the flow abruptly stopped.

Lily's gaze remained fixed on the window, taking in the blurriness and a clear handprint in the center. She crept toward it and placed her hand against the glass.

The size perfectly matched the handprint of La Llorona.

Chapter 7

Lily woke just after sunrise the next morning, the first to get up. Later, when Lencha shuffled into the kitchen still wearing her robe, Lily registered the change in her aunt's appearance.

Her dark eyes, usually bright and lively, were now dull. Instead of her signature neat braid, her hair was loose, and it looked like she hadn't bothered to brush it.

Lily guided her to a chair. Lencha sat with her head in her hands.

At the sink, Lily poured water into a pan and set it on the stove, turning the flame to high. What they both needed, badly, was a cafecito.

The kitchen curtains were closed, but through the thin fabric, Lily watched the outlines of people walking along the narrow pathway between the houses, making their way toward Lencha's shed and her remedies. Lily quickly told her aunt what she'd seen in the night.

Lencha groaned. "This is a terrible time for me to get sick, with Catalina gone. And I haven't even had time to teach you anything."

Lily scooped coffee grounds into the aluminum jug and added boiling water.

"I'll try to get off early today. Plus, I have tomorrow and Monday off because my boss wants me to work next weekend. There must be something I can do."

Lencha smiled weakly.

Lily knew it had taken Lencha most of her lifetime to learn her skills. What could she possibly teach Lily in a few days? Certainly not enough to help all those desperate people outside.

Lily stared at the brown paper bag where she'd left it on the table. She pulled out the scissors and held them up. "Can I do something with these?"

The question seemed to exhaust Lencha, who fell back in her chair, shoulders slumping. "Ay, Lily. It's too bad your father didn't let you come to me when you were younger, like I asked. We wouldn't be in the mess we're in now if he hadn't been so darn stubborn."

Lily felt a pang of guilt for not taking it upon herself to visit her aunt—alone, unmarried, and without any other family. She'd hardly given Lencha a thought growing up. But at least she was here now. And Lily was willing to do whatever she could to help the people of Chavez Ravine.

She pushed her shoulders back, set the scissors on the table, and turned to Lencha. "You can show me when I get back from work. But first, I'm going to tell all those people out there to go home because you need to get back in bed and get some rest." When Lencha opened her mouth to argue, Lily shook her head. "The healer needs to heal. They'll just have to wait a bit."

Lily hurried outside to deliver the bad news. There was a bit of grumbling, but mostly, they understood and dispersed, casting worried glances at the house as they went. But others would come, and when they didn't find Lencha in her shed, they'd knock on the door.

Lily thought for a moment, then went back inside, found a piece of cardboard, and wrote a note both in English and Spanish. She tacked it onto the door of the shed, then made a second one and affixed it to the front door.

When she was done, Lily went back into the house. Lencha's coughing had worsened.

"Is there anything I can do for you before I leave?" Lily asked with concern.

Lencha nodded. From her bed, she explained how to make an ointment to soothe her cough. In the kitchen, Lily mixed an egg white with olive oil. Lencha swallowed a teaspoon and smeared some on her neck and chest.

Before Lily left, Lencha pointed to the only other piece of furniture in the room: an ancient dresser made of dark wood.

"There's a necklace in the top drawer," Lencha said between coughs.

It was easy to find. Only one piece of jewelry sat in the drawer, atop a folded piece of cloth. It was a small rough stone. A thin wire wrapped around it and attached to a simple chain.

Lily was bringing it over to Lencha when her aunt held up her hand.

"It's not for me. It's for you. A little protection to help keep La Llorona away. It used to belong to my mother. I wore it as a child, and now it's yours."

Touched by her aunt's thoughtfulness, Lily held the necklace in her palm, feeling generations of protection in the simple black stone. She clasped it around her neck, the pendant resting against the skin of her chest.

"Thank you, Tia." Lily spoke softly, voice filled with emotion.

Lencha leaned back against her pillows. "You're a good girl, Lily. And you're real smart. We'll do the best we can do. On your way home, can you stop at the botanica on Bishop Road and buy some red string? Tonight, I'll show you how to make protection bracelets."

"Of course, I can. It's right on my way home."

Lencha coughed loudly. "Good. At least we'll have those when people show up tomorrow. Now get going before you're late."

Lily hurried down the long and crooked path toward the streetcar, clutching the little black stone, the events of the last twenty-four hours replaying in her mind.

Chapter 8

The morning seemed to drag on at the garment factory. It was cooler than the day before but still warm for fall, once again hotter inside the building than out. A pregnant seamstress fainted at her sewing machine. When she recovered, Lily helped her to the bathroom and pressed damp rags to the back of her neck.

"I can ask the boss if you could go home early," Lily offered.

The young woman, named Carol, shook her head. "No. I'd have to take the streetcar and walk all the way home. My husband is going to pick me up after work."

Lily cranked open the casement window to let in some air. "Where do you live?"

"Up in Palo Verde."

"In Chavez Ravine? I just moved to La Loma to live with my aunt. Lencha Bantacorte."

"The bruja?"

Lily was surprised to hear Carol call Lencha a witch, rather than a healer. "That's her."

"I've been feeling sick to my stomach, but the curandera in Palo Verde went to see some family." Carol fanned herself. "Maybe your aunt can help me. My husband can give you a ride home, and maybe I can see her then?"

Lily shook her head. "That's not a good idea. She's got a cold or something. You don't want to catch what she has."

"Can she tell you how to fix something up for me?"

"I don't know," Lily said uncertainly. "Maybe. We can check." No harm would come from asking. And the ride would help her avoid the streetcar and another run-in with La Llorona.

After Carol splashed cold water on her face, Lily escorted her back to the big room where the seamstresses worked, crowded together and surrounded by bins spilling over with fabric.

She was walking back to the office when she suddenly stopped.

Goosebumps prickled Lily's skin. An unsettling presence that did not belong lingered in the busy room, amidst the rhythmic whirring of sewing machines and the creaking of the foot pedals moving up and down.

Lily slowly turned, eyes scanning the space.

She jumped back with a gasp.

There, high up in a corner, where the light from the small windows barely reached, a shrouded figure perched like a giant spider, its limbs outstretched and body pressed against the ceiling.

A flowing white veil obscured the figure's face, but Lily could still make out skeletal features and black empty eye sockets staring right at her. It only vaguely resembled the apparition which had haunted her in the streetcar, but it was La Llorona.

The seamstresses continued their work, oblivious to the terrifying thing looming above.

Then Lily remembered the protection necklace Lencha had given her. With trembling fingers, she grasped the stone. A surge of energy coursed through her, and she brandished the black stone at La Llorona. The ghostly figure let out an ear-splitting scream and thrashed wildly, its white veil billowing like a sail in a storm.

Behind Lily, the sewing machines fell silent.

By the expressions on their startled faces, the women had heard the scream but seemed confused about where it had come from.

"What was that?" a quavering voice asked in Spanish.

"It sounded like La Llorona," replied Carol. "She was up in Palo Verde last night, and that's what she sounded like."

Lily slumped against the doorway, watching the women cross themselves.

A moment later, Mr. Whitaker appeared in the hallway, eyes wide above his five o'clock shadow. "Did someone scream?"

Lily froze, and the seamstresses exchanged nervous glances. Their boss wasn't half as bad as others in the garment district, but he was a gringo, and he would just think they were superstitious fools..

"A machine acted up, and one of the girls jabbed her finger," Lily lied.

Across the room, Carol made a show of grimacing and wrapping a piece of cloth around her finger. That seemed to satisfy Mr. Whitaker. He gave a curt nod and strode back toward his office.

When he was gone, the women broke into frenzied chatter. The weeping woman was known to haunt quiet, lonely places, wandering through arroyos, riverbeds, cemeteries, even alleyways and darkened streets, but never a busy workplace.

Still shaking, Lily told them to keep it down, then hurried back to her desk, clutching her necklace and hoping it was enough to keep the crying lady away.

Chapter 9

Lily stepped out into the bright daylight, Carol at her side. Immediately, she noticed Emiliano leaning against his old Ford. Even from that distance, the man seemed annoyed he hadn't found her alone.

Lily was seized by the sudden urge to scream at him, "Go away! Leave me alone!" Had her mother sent him to plead with her to return?

Carol was too busy talking about La Llorona to notice the man across the street, watching them. An old Dodge pulled up in front of the curb, and the two ladies climbed in.

By the time they'd stopped at the botanica, where Lily bought a large bag stuffed with red string, she regretted accepting the ride. Carol's husband had a baby face, but he acted just like Emiliano—the way he stared at her when Carol wasn't looking, the winks, the licking of his pouty lips when he tried to catch Lily's eye in the rearview mirror.

Carol seemed oblivious to her husband's wandering eyes. Lily wondered how long they'd been married. Some men, she'd heard, didn't like sharing their wife's attention with a new baby and so flirted with other women.

But that was no excuse. Lily was disgusted and could hardly bring herself to look at him. She and Carol made arrangements to meet the next morning. Hopefully, that would give Lily time to learn how to make something for Carol's morning sickness.

But inside, she found Lencha still in bed, sicker than when Lily had left her.

"I'm no good at curing myself," Lencha muttered.

Lily didn't like the sound of her aunt's wet, phlegmy cough. "Maybe we should get you a doctor. Is there one here in Chavez Ravine?"

Lencha smiled. "Ay, no. Then why would anyone need me?" She paused. "There *is* a doctor. A good one. Down in Chinatown. But I'm not sick enough to bother him. I'll be fine in a few days." Sitting up in bed took some effort. Lencha coughed and frowned in Lily's direction. "I can see it on your face. La Llorona showed up again, didn't she?"

Reluctantly—she hated to trouble her aunt while Lencha was so sick—Lily shared her story, then groaned. "Why is she following me? What does she want?"

Lencha stared up at the ceiling, blinking slowly. "Maybe she's trying to tell you something," she finally said.

"Like what?"

Lencha shrugged. "I don't know. Maybe she was trying to tell you to pay attention."

"Pay attention to what?" Lily's voice was shrill.

Lencha sighed heavily. "It's just a feeling I have."

The cryptic answer left Lily feeling unsettled, but there was no point in pestering the woman. Plus Lily needed to learn how to make the red string protection bracelets and the morning sickness cure.

Lily went into the kitchen to heat up some caldo de pollo. The chicken soup revived Lencha.

Lily brought a small table and chair into Lencha's bedroom. At first, the string felt stiff and thick and seemed to resist her attempts to form the tiny knots, but eventually, Lily got the hang of it and fell into the rhythm of the work.

"It's best to do this on a Tuesday," Lencha said. "But we can't wait around until then."

Lily paused, glancing up. Her aunt looked worried.

"Why Tuesday?"

"I don't know. It's something my mother always said. The ones we made on Tuesdays worked better."

While Lencha shared stories of her youth in Mexico, Lily blessed the bracelets with holy water, trying to remember the last time she had gone to church. Lencha assured her it didn't matter. Lily didn't think the priests she'd met would agree, and she told Lencha as much.

Her aunt snorted. "This has nothing to do with them," she said dismissively, then instructed Lily to light a stick of copal incense and run the finished bracelets through the smoke.

The bracelets were intended for the children of worried parents, Lencha explained.

The next project involved making bolsitas—little charm bags for protection. Lily was relieved to learn they did not require tiresome knots. She just needed to collect some items from the shed.

Afterward, her aunt took her by surprise when she told Lily to go into the kitchen, close the curtains, and organize everything on the wooden table.

"Just sit back, relax, and concentrate. And then you'll light a candle and say a prayer."

Lily stiffened. "Tia, I'm not a very good Catholic."

Lencha rolled her eyes. "Did I say you needed to be a good Catholic?"

"No," Lily admitted.

"Do you see a priest in here, telling you what to do?"

"No."

"And you want to help these people, don't you? You said you did, and I believe you can. Sometimes, that's all a bruja needs. Faith in herself. And even if you *don't* believe in yourself yet, I do."

Lily nodded. Lencha sounded so sure. For now, that would have to do.

In the kitchen, Lily carried out the rest of Lencha's instructions. To each little red sachet bag, she added a small black stone, a medal made of tin, a dried leaf from a plant Lencha called epazote, and three peonia seeds, which Lencha warned her not to accidentally break because the insides were poisonous.

When she was done, Lily pulled the drawstrings and cinched the bags closed, tying them off with a special knot. After a sprinkling of holy water, she said the prayer Lencha had scribbled on a piece of paper.

Her next project took her outside. Following Lencha's instructions, Lily dug up a dozen small aloe plants and carried them into the shed. She brushed the dirt off the roots, then tied a length of red string around the base of each plant.

It was late afternoon when Lily finally finished. After a quick cafecito, she began making deliveries around La Loma.

Lily's first stop was at Betty's house. Betty came to the door wearing an apron made from flour sacks.

From the aroma wafting out of the kitchen, Lily guessed Betty had been making enchiladas. Lily's stomach grumbled. Betty waved her inside.

"Come in, come in. Have a little something to eat. You look worn out."

Lily was tempted, but she shook her head. "Thank you, but I just came to drop this off." She pulled an aloe plant out of the basket hanging from her arm.

Betty wrinkled her forehead and squinted at the plant, then looked back at Lily and murmured, "Hmmm."

It was obvious what she was thinking.

"My aunt told me what to do," Lily said briskly, with more confidence than she felt.

A nail already protruded from the door, white paint chipping off to reveal the wood underneath. Lily hung the plant upside down, hooking the red string around the nail.

Betty stood back to inspect the results. "That looks all right," she finally said.

The woman didn't sound convinced, but there was no helping that. Betty peered into Lily's overflowing basket, eyes widening.

"You weren't planning on delivering all those tonight were you?" When Lily nodded, Betty said, "It'll be dark! You don't want to be out alone after sundown, not with La Llorona around."

Before Lily could reply, Betty was hanging over the porch railing and shouting at the house next door.

"Hey, Sal! Get on out here."

A few moments later, the screen door banged open and Sal appeared, still wearing work clothes covered in grime. "Come on, Betty. I was just about to get cleaned up."

When he noticed Lily, his expression softened. "Lily! What are you doing here? I heard Lencha was sick. Is everything okay?"

Lily was touched by the big man's concern.

Betty didn't give her a chance to reply. She pointed to Lily's basket and huffed. "Liliana plans on gallivanting around La Loma, like Little Red Riding Hood with the wolf on the loose. I think that's a bad idea, and I think you should go with her to make sure she's safe."

Sal rubbed the side of his face, then seemed to make up his mind. "I'm not sure I'll be much good against La Llorona, but Betty's right, for once. This isn't something you should do alone."

Lily felt a surge of gratitude. With everyone holed up in their houses, too afraid to go outside, the streets were deserted. And Lily didn't know the area yet. Having Sal along would be a big help.

"Thank you, Sal. That's so nice of you."

With that, they set off. Sal regaled her with stories about La Llorona he'd heard from his stop at the liquor store.

The weeping woman had terrorized the gringo bachelors in the one-room shacks on the hill stretching down to Solano Canyon. On Bishop Road in Palo Verde, La Llorona had suddenly materialized in front of a man pulling a fruit cart. He was so startled, he tipped over the cart, spilling limes and lemons onto the street. A group of boys racing down a hill on their carritos swore they saw La Llorona floating in the air, and they had gotten so scared, one of them crashed into a cactus.

"And the crazy thing is," Sal concluded, "La Llorona has never been seen around here before. Over in Elysian Park? Sure. Down in the Solano neighborhood? Sure. And a bunch of other places too. But here? Never."

Once again, Lily had the feeling Sal suspected her of drawing La Llorona to the neighborhood. The weight of the unspoken accusation niggled at her while they walked the streets of La Loma.

At every house, they left an aloe plant and a red-string bracelet for each child. Lily had to continuously reassure the residents that while Lencha had been too sick to do the hechizos herself, Lily had carefully followed her aunt's instructions.

When they reached the last few houses, the wind picked up, causing the power lines overhead to hum.

Sal looked around nervously. "Let's get you home."

They quickened their pace. Frightened eyes watched them from the windows. Just as they turned the corner onto Lencha's street, a thick fog dropped from the sky, swirling around them, enveloping the street and yards in a ghostly shroud.

"What bullshit is this?" Sal muttered.

The fog was so heavy, it was difficult to see even a few feet. Lily knew Lencha's house couldn't be far, yet it might have been miles. She'd lost all sense of direction.

"I think Lencha's place is over there." Sal took Lily's elbow, pulling her through the whiteness.

The massive palm tree next to Lencha's house loomed into view, a monstrous silhouette. The fog muffled their footsteps. At the end of a lane, a dog began to howl. Lily desperately wanted to be inside, away from the damp white murk clinging to her skin and hair.

She clutched her now-empty basket. "Do you think La Llorona is doing this?" Lily couldn't make out Sal's expression through the fog.

"I don't know, but we're not going to wait around to find out."

And then they were stumbling up a short flight of stairs. Lily opened the door, and they both went in.

The house was eerily quiet. Lily motioned for Sal to stay in the living room and hurried toward Lencha's bedroom.

Her aunt was asleep, hidden beneath a mound of blankets. Lily pulled back the cover and felt her aunt's forehead with the back of her hand. It was burning hot. Lily was tempted to wake Lencha and ask if there was anything she could do to bring down her fever, but she decided not to disturb her.

Sometimes, sleep was the best medicine.

Lily returned to the living room. Sal was standing at the front window, staring outside, his shoulders hunched up around his ears. The man was so big, the room seemed smaller with him in it.

Lily went into the kitchen and came out holding the last two aloe plants. There was no need to hammer in any nails. Both the front door and side door had them, and Lily quickly hung the plants with Sal looking on, nodding in approval.

"Let's hope those work," Sal said, collapsing into the only chair in the room. "And if they don't, at least we have Lencha."

Sal didn't seem to have any intention of leaving. Not that Lily blamed him. She wouldn't want to venture outside either. The fog pressed against the windows as if trying to get in.

Lily cleared her throat. "I don't think Lencha's going to be much help tonight. She's got a fever."

Sal tipped his head back and groaned. "That's bad." He seemed to sink deeper into his chair, taking in the cozy room. "What I could really use is a drink."

"My aunt doesn't have any liquor in the house," Lily said primly. She wanted Sal to stay sober and alert until the strange fog was gone.

Sal barked out a harsh laugh. "Then you don't know your tia. Of course she does. She *always* has some tequila around. Just in case her man friend comes to visit."

"What man friend?" Lily blinked.

Lencha hadn't said anything about having a boyfriend. Then again, there hadn't been much time for chit-chat.

"A gringo. That's all I know. I've seen him a couple of times, but Lencha, she doesn't like people knowing her business."

Sal waved his hand in the direction of the kitchen.

"I don't want to go snooping through her stuff, but if you look hard enough, you'll find it." When he registered Lily's hesitation, he added, "I was supposed to go to a party in Bishop tonight. My novia is not going to be too happy with me when I don't show up."

So Sal had a girlfriend. For some reason, that made Lily like the man even more.

"She wouldn't want you to go out in this, with everything that's going on. Bishop's on the other side of Palo Verde, isn't it?"

"It is." Sal gave a heavy sigh. "I wonder if the fog is over there too?" He sounded worried.

Lily wished more people in Chavez Ravine had phones. Sal got up and began pacing around, lost in his own thoughts.

Lily went into the kitchen. If the man wanted a drink, she owed him that. He'd chaperoned her around La Loma, and now he was stuck at Lencha's house with her instead of dancing with his girlfriend. And since he was staying, she might as well figure out dinner and find some extra blankets.

After a few glasses of tequila, full from the makeshift meal Lily had fixed with leftovers from the icebox, Sal passed out on a cot she set up in the living room.

Lily quietly went into Lencha's bedroom. She sat down on a chair, huddled beneath a blanket, and watched her aunt's slow breathing. Even though Lencha was sick, Lily felt safer being in the same room. The ticking clock eventually soothed her jangly nerves, and she dozed off.

Sometime in the night, through a haze of sleep, Lily thought she heard the distant sound of wailing. A cry laced with anger. Or maybe it was frustration. But it came no closer.

Lily thought of the aloe plants and smiled. They must have been working after all.

Chapter 10

When she woke up, Sal was nowhere to be found. The fog continued to hang in the air, but it was thinner than the night before. Still, Lily could barely see the street through the hazy mist.

At least she had the day off from work. And Monday too.

Lencha slept on, her labored breathing muffled under the blankets. Lily frowned, feeling a knot of anxiety form in her chest. She gently placed a hand on her aunt's forehead and winced at the heat radiating from her skin.

Lily rushed to the kitchen and grabbed a few clean rags and a bowl of cool water. She placed one on Lencha's forehead and used the others to wipe down her neck and arms. Lencha's nightgown was drenched with sweat, so Lily searched through the dresser for a fresh one. When she turned back, Lencha was struggling to sit up.

"Did she come back?" Lencha rasped, her eyes searching Lily's face for an answer.

"I don't think so." Lily supported her aunt while Lencha changed into the clean nightgown.

A small, satisfied smile spread across Lencha's face. "The hechizos worked, then."

Lily helped her aunt to the bathroom and then into the kitchen, where Lencha sat down heavily in a chair. Lily bustled around, and soon the kitchen was filled with the comforting aroma of freshly brewed coffee. The sizzle of chilaquiles on the stove added spice to the air.

Lily's mother made the dish with green chili, but Lily preferred red sauce made with tomatoes, chicken broth, and smoky dried chilis pasillas. She was relieved her aunt had an appetite. Lencha ate half of the plate of chilaquiles Lily served her.

After finishing her second cup of coffee with plenty of milk and sugar, Lencha appeared more alert and gazed toward the kitchen window. The curtains were still closed, blocking the view.

"The light looks funny," she remarked with narrowed eyes.

Lily pulled back the curtains to reveal the mist outside. "It's fog. It's been like this since last night. It got so bad Sal Martinez had to stay over."

With her eyes still focused on the window, Lencha spoke in a distant tone. "He's a good man. Did you see La Llorona before the fog came?"

Lily shook her head. "No, I didn't."

"Let's hope this is a coincidence." Lencha coughed. "That fog will make it harder for people to see her. And if they don't see her, they may not be able to get away from her."

Lily poured herself another cup of coffee. "I think people are too scared to go out."

She was soon proven wrong. People began to file past the window, headed for the backyard.

When her aunt struggled to stand, Lily held up a hand. "Now that you showed me what to do, why don't you let me take over today? You need to rest."

"Ay, but Lily—" Lencha began to cough.

"Please, Aunt. You're in no condition to work today. I can make bracelets and bolsitas. And there are lots more aloe plants in the yard. I'm no curandera, but I can help calm jittery nerves."Lencha looked at Lily through watery eyes. "You're more of a curandera than you think, mija. And you came at just the right time, Lily. Thank you."

Lily didn't reply. Instead, she leaned down and kissed her aunt on the cheek. "I'm glad to be here."

And she meant it. Even with La Llorona in Chavez Ravine, her mother's house—with Emiliano—was a scarier place to be.

And then she remembered Carol.

She hadn't come by to get help with her morning sickness.

Chapter 11

The shed was freezing, thanks to the damp and chilly fog enveloping it. But Lily hardly felt the cold, all bundled up in an old coat belonging to Lencha.

The task at hand demanded her full attention. La Llorona had been seen roaming near the police academy, so parents had walked all the way from Palo Verde and Bishop, seeking protection bracelets for their children.

People told story after story about La Lorona.

She had been heard wailing on Effie Street, right in front of the grocery store.

High in the hills of Bishop, a man had seen a massive creature draped in a white shroud, at least eight feet tall, coming toward him. Its eyes were a piercing red, and its teeth were long, like a vampire's. He ran inside his house and slammed the door shut behind him. Moments later, rocks began pelting against the windows of his house.

The fog took its time spreading through Bishop and Palo Verde, but from what Lily heard, it had reached most of the streets in Chavez Ravine: Davis, Curtis, Malvina, Aqua Pura Drive, all the way to Boylston Street, leading out of Bishop into Los Angeles. But the strange fog was confined to the three villages in the ravine.

By eleven o'clock, Lily had run out of red string, and the aloe plants in the garden were nearly gone. Betty arrived with a platter of taquitos for lunch and said when Sal returned from work, they could gather some aloe plants from the garden belonging to Catalina, the bruja who was away.

"Won't she mind?" Lily asked.

Betty clucked her tongue and pushed a taquito toward Lily.

"Ay, no. They help each other all the time. Eat quick because I need you to come with me. Some kids saw La Llorona last night, and now they've got such a bad case of susto, they can't stop crying." When Betty registered Lily's stricken expression, she added, "They didn't have any bracelets. The parents think they're too good for that sort of stuff. But *now* they want help."

The solution involved a sweeping ritual. Lily listened to Lencha's instructions, but by her expression, Lily knew her aunt wasn't sure she could do it.

Lily put some supplies from the shed into a bag, then she and Betty went to see the frightened children. When their mother answered the door, she seemed disapproving. But the children, still cowering in their beds, were happy to see her.

Lily went to work.

She pulled a bundle of rosemary stems from her bag and, one by one, brushed each child from head to toe with the fragrant plants. Then she rubbed an egg on their faces and arms and cracked it into a glass of water.

Lily held the glass up to the light and peered at the contents. A real curandera would know what to look for and could tell what was bothering the patients by the appearance of the yolk. But to Lily, it just looked like an egg in water. Besides, she already knew what was bothering the children: they'd seen La Lorona.

Finally, Lily mixed a bit of sugar in a jug of warm water, poured a glass for each child, and told them to drink up. When she was done, the color had returned to their ashen faces, and they climbed out of their beds.

By the time Lily left, carrying a stack of tortillas and a pound of frijoles in her bag, their mother's attitude had improved dramatically.

Lily returned to Lencha's house. There, pacing back and forth on the porch, was Carol.

"Is everything okay?" Lily called, rushing toward her.

Carol's sweater was stretched over her pregnant stomach, buttoned all wrong. Her hair, usually neatly pinned up, fell over her shoulders in loose, unbrushed waves.

She shook her head, eyes wide. "Johnny didn't come home last night. I'm so scared, Lily. The fog was so bad. What if something happened to him? I don't know what to do."

Carol didn't mention La Llorona, but Lily knew that's what worried her friend the most.

"Where did Johnny go?" Lily asked, even though she could guess the answer. Whatever it was, it probably involved another woman.

Carol bit her lip and looked away. "He went to see some buddies. There was a house party, I think."

"In Bishop?"

Tears welled in Carol's eyes. "Yes."

Probably the same party Sal was supposed to go to before the fog came in.

As if summoned, a truck roared up. Sal hopped out and strode toward them, still dressed in his work clothes. "Betty told me to get over here and—"

His words died on his lips when he spotted Carol. "You two know each other?"

"We work together," Lily rushed to explain. "Carol says her husband didn't come home last night."

Sal rubbed the side of face. "Maybe La Llorona got him."

Carol burst into tears.

"Sal!" Lily scolded.

Sal didn't look the least bit sorry. "What was that damn fool husband of yours doing leaving you solita, expecting a baby and everything, with that she-devil on the loose?"

Carol swiped at her eyes with a sniff. "He needs to get out once in a while."

"It's a lot more than once in a while, from what I hear," Sal replied dryly.

Lily shot Sal a stern look, then guided Carol inside. She reheated some coffee, adding extra milk to Carol's cup, then fried some eggs and put them on top of the leftover chilaquiles. They could eat while they talked about what to do.

Sal dabbed his mouth with a napkin and sat back in his chair. He gave Lily an apologetic look before turning to Carol. "Is there any chance Johnny could be at Nina's house?"

Carol's nostrils flared. "He doesn't see her anymore."

Sal gave Carol a look that said he didn't believe it. Lily didn't have to ask who Nina was—she sounded like old trouble.

"Sometimes he stays out late, but he's always home by morning." Carol took small bites of the food on her plate. "That's why I'm so worried."

Sal began to look uneasy. "Well, La Llorona kept her distance from La Loma last night, but it sounds like she caused plenty of trouble in Palo Verde and Bishop."

"That's true. I barely slept a wink with all her screaming and crying."

Carol did look exhausted, Lily thought to herself. "Sal, maybe we should drive around to see if we can find him. Or his car."

Sal rubbed an eyebrow, frowning. "I guess so. But if I find that pinche cabron at Nina's, I'm going to give it to him good."

After settling Carol on the couch in the living room, blanket tucked around her legs, Lily and Sal left.

The fog was hanging on. It wasn't as thick as the day before, but the persisting mist was strange. It seemed to slither around the cacti, wild rose bushes, and houses, turning everything into a sad, fading landscape. It was almost like the houses had been abandoned—the once lively streets devoid of activity in the swirling mist.

Lily sat next to Sal, brow furrowed, gazing out at the desolate neighborhood of La Loma. The truck bumped along the rutted dirt roads.

"Why don't you have any sidewalks up here?" Lily asked.

Sal snorted. "Because those pendejos at the city won't put them in. Betty and a group of ladies organized a committee, and they've asked and asked and asked, but nothing ever gets done."

They zig-zagged through the streets. Sal kept up a commentary about the people who inhabited the houses.

"That's where the Rivas family lives. That one belongs to the Flores. See that big one? Manny Contreras bought it with cash from some gringo in Pasadena who owns a bunch of properties around here. Paid for it with the money he made with his tortilla factories."

Lily looked out the window. The house was big—two stories tall and twice the size of the others on the street. And just a few doors up, where the block ended, she spotted Johnny's Dodge.

Sal let out a low whistle. "That's what I was afraid of. Looks like we found Johnny." He pointed at a rundown cottage with peeling paint and overgrown bushes. "That's where Nina lives with her abuela. Her parents live in Bishop, and they're real strict. When they found out she was seeing Johnny, they kicked her out."

"Does her grandmother know about Johnny?"

"She's too soft, that woman. She believes everything Nina tells her."

The cottage's windows were dark. Sal parked, and Lily trailed behind, making her way up the weed-choked path. The fog was thicker and seemed to cling to them.

Sal knocked. No one came to the door. The houses on either side also had a vacant air.

"No one seems to be home," Lily said.

Sal's eyebrows lifted, and he smacked his forehead. "Oh. It's Sunday morning. They probably went to mass. To the church in Palo Verde. Mass at ten, then menudo afterward."

Lily nodded. That explained why they hadn't received any visitors seeking help that morning.

She surveyed the area, the porch floorboards creaking under her feet. Where the street ended, a barren hill rose into the fog, power lines crisscrossing overhead. She could just make out an odd shape at the top of the hill.

"What's up there?"

Sal followed her gaze. "An old well. During the day, the kids like to go up there and play, ride their carritos down. At night, that's where couples go to mess around. Don't ask me why. The back of a car is more comfortable."

Suddenly, Lily wanted to see it for herself. She started up the hill, the damp fog enveloping her like a cold, wet blanket. Sal called after her, but she pressed on, her curiosity getting the better of her. Lily clutched the black stone hanging from the chain around her neck, just in case.

Was it her imagination, or had the fog thickened? She could barely see more than a few yards in front of her. The well came into view. The lid was off, lying on the ground as if someone had tossed it aside.

She peered over the edge. It wasn't very deep—maybe twelve feet or so. Something at the bottom caught her eye, something coiled at the bottom. Heart beating faster, Lily squinted, trying to make it out, and gasped.

It was a man half submerged in a foot of water.

Sal appeared next to Lily, panting. He leaned over the side and jumped back. "What the hell is Johnny doing in there?"

"I don't know," Lily stammered. She stared at the motionless figure below, and a chill ran down her spine.

A sudden rush of wind swept across the hill, disrupting the mist. Shadows seemed to shift in the unnatural light. The trees on the ridge at Elysian Park swayed wildly.

In the distance, a low moan echoed through the fog.

Sal clutched her arm. "Did you hear that?"

Before Lily could reply, the moan became a piercing wail which sounded like it was getting closer.

In silent agreement, they bolted down the slope toward the truck.

Chapter 12

While Sal sped through the streets of La Loma, Lily turned around in her seat. A ghostly figure flew through the air in pursuit, but when Lily brandished her black stone necklace in the apparition's direction, it disappeared.

They returned to Lencha's house, where Sal broke the news to Carol. She immediately burst into tears but, after a few minutes of sobbing, regained her composure.

It seemed to Lily Carol should have been more upset, all the more since she had a baby on the way. But maybe Carol knew more about Johnny's ways than she let on so her grief was more bearable.

Life with Johnny couldn't have been easy, and things were only going to get harder once the baby came. Carol must have known that.

"I don't want to call the police," Carol said when her tears had dried.

No one objected.

Sal said he'd get a group together to retrieve Johnny's body. When he and Carol had gone, Lencha walked into the living room, still wearing her slippers and wrapped in a blanket. She sat on the couch while Lily told her what had happened.

"So Johnny has to be with that other woman even when La Llorona is all over the place? Idiot." Lencha muttered. "What was he thinking, leaving his pregnant wife alone?"

Lily remembered the way Johnny had looked at her while his wife was just a few feet away. "I think he was the type to have only one thing on his mind. Poor Carol."

Lencha leaned back against the pillows. "She's better off. He wasn't going to be any help anyway." Lencha's eyes narrowed. "My mother used to say La Llorona appears to people who've wronged others. Sometimes, she takes revenge. Johnny was up to no good, cheating on his wife. La Llorona had man troubles of her own, so what happened to him doesn't surprise me."

"But what does she want with the rest of us? We may not be perfect, but most of us don't need punishing. But she's here anyway."

Lencha shrugged and let out a heavy sigh.

Lily was relieved her aunt was looking more alert. After giving Lencha the rest of the chicken soup and spearmint tea, she sent Lencha off to bed and tidied the kitchen. She was too unsettled to read a book, so she spent the rest of the afternoon giving the house a good cleaning and washing clothes on the back porch.

It was still too damp outside to hang them on the clothesline, so Lily draped them around the kitchen chairs and on a rack she found in the pantry. Lily guessed her aunt used the rack to dry herbs, but it would do.

When the sun started to set, Sal knocked on the door and delivered an aluminum-covered tray of enchiladas from Betty. He'd taken care of Johnny's body.

That was enough for Lily. She didn't ask for more details.

The evening stretched on. Lily washed her hair and painted her nails, frequently peering out the windows to see if anything was stirring in the mist.

After dinner, Lily made hot chocolate with cinnamon and sat in a chair next to a dozing Lencha's bed. By ten o'clock, Lencha's fever had returned.

To Lily's surprise, Lencha awoke just before midnight and insisted on moving into the living room, where she slumped on the sofa.

"Get your scissors, Lily," she wheezed. "We need to consecrate them if they're going to do you any good."

Lily fetched the scissors from the kitchen. "What does that mean?"

"It's kind of like a dedication." Lencha pointed to a small table. "Put them there for now. I need you to bring me some other things."

In five minutes, Lily had set out all the items on a lace doily: a clay bowl, some beans, several sage leaves, a vial of holy water, a small jagged black stone, and a clean rag.

"Put your scissors in the bowl," Lencha commanded.

Lencha's lips began to move, and Lily realized she was praying. But it was a prayer unlike any she'd heard before. Lencha prayed about demons and sorcerers, then for the sharp edges of the blades to cut the ill intentions of Lily's enemies.

Lily immediately thought of Emiliano.

"Now, take those scissors outside and expose them to the night sky."

"What if La Llorona takes them?" Lily asked, opening the side door.

Lencha frowned. "She's good at scaring people, not stealing things. Now don't go ruin everything we just did. Put them outside and bring them in before dawn."

Lencha yawned, followed by a coughing fit.

Lily put the scissors on the porch rail, then came back inside and locked the door. Lencha had gone back to her bedroom.

Lily was afraid to go to bed, worried she'd sleep through dawn and ruin the consecration of the scissors. She slipped off her shoes but didn't change out of her clothes. Didn't want to get too comfortable.

For hours, she lay in her small bed, staring up at the ceiling, listening for any strange noises from outside. But all was quiet. The fog had once again thickened, muffling every sound.

She was starting to doze off when a crash echoed through the house, causing her to bolt out of bed. Someone was banging on the front door.

Mouth dry, heart slamming against her rib cage, Lily tiptoed into the living room, ignoring Lencha's startled cry from the bedroom.

The banging continued, rattling the door in its hinges. Whoever was out there had no intention of going away. Lily crept to the window and peered out between a gap in the curtains.

It was dark outside and still foggy, but she immediately recognized the burly outline of her stepfather.

"Open this goddamn door, Liliana!"

From the way he was slurring his words, she knew he was drunk.

Lily dashed into Lencha's room. "I'm going to get my scissors," she hissed.

Lencha grabbed her by the wrist. "They won't do you any good. Not until morning. And I'll be no good at getting rid of him. Not in my condition. Go get Sal. He'll take care of him."

At the front of the house, Emiliano continued to yell. "You're coming home with me now, puta."

Lily didn't blame the neighbors for not coming to investigate. Not with the fog. Not with La Llorona out there. Not with a crazy man, probably dangerous, shouting filth. But she didn't have a choice. If she didn't act, he'd break down the door or a window and give her a good beating before he dragged her home.

Panic rose in Lily's chest. "What if he gets inside while I'm gone?"

"He's not here for me," Lencha said firmly. "Vayanse."

Lily nodded, then sprinted for the side door. Emiliano was still making too much of a racket for him to hear any small noise she might make. She was halfway across the yard when she realized she'd forgotten to put on shoes, but it was too late for that.

What if Emiliano got back in his car and left? He'd drive right by her, and God only knew what would happen then. And what if La Llorona appeared? Lily suddenly felt exposed and vulnerable. She choked back a sob and continued running.

When she arrived at Sal's house, sweat had plastered her blouse to her skin. She knocked on the door, glancing back, half expecting Emiliano to appear right behind her.

A light flicked on in the living room, and then the door creaked open. Sal stood in the doorway, shirtless and scratching his stomach. But when his sleepy eyes registered Lily, he snapped awake.

"What's wrong? Is Lencha all right?"

Lily burst into tears. "She's fine. It's my stepfather. He's at the house. He's a bad man, Sal, and he's going to take me with him."

Sal didn't reply. He shoved his feet into a pair of dirty work boots on the porch.

"Like hell he is." Sal jerked his head in the direction of the living room. "You stay here. I'll deal with the cabron. I'll be back as soon as I can."

Lily wanted to go with him, but Sal wouldn't hear of it, so she went inside and closed the door. The living room was small, with just two leather armchairs, a round table, and several framed photos hanging high on the wall. The room smelled of stale cigarettes, but at least it was clean, and the chair was deep and comfortable.

It felt like an eternity passed before Sal stomped on the porch. Lily rushed to the door and looked him up and down for signs of damage.

"What happened?"

Sal rubbed the side of his face and scowled. "I told that pendejo if he came back, he'd be sorry. Then I threw him into his car and watched him leave La Loma. If he doesn't crash on the way home, it will be a miracle. He was out-of-his-mind borracho."

Sal stared down at Lily, frown deepening.

"You're not a little girl. You've got a good job and everything. What does he want with you?"

When Lily looked away, a surge of heat rising to her cheeks, Sal's expression hardened.

"Oh. He's one of those, huh? His own wife isn't good enough. He's got to have the daughter too? Well, he better not come back. Not if he knows what's good for him." Sal slammed his enormous fist into the palm of his plate-sized hand. "Now, let's get you home."

Minutes later, still trembling, Lily let herself inside the side door of Lencha's house. A rooster crowed next door. It was nearly dawn.

Chapter 13

The fog and Lencha's stubborn fever both lingered into the early morning. Lily was pressing cold wet cloths against Lencha's forehead when she remembered the scissors. They were still outside.

Lily peered out the windows, looking for any signs of Emiliano or La Llorona in the dim, early light. Not seeing anything, she darted out the side door to retrieve them.

She recalled the prayer of consecration and wondered if the scissors could be used to cut out Lencha's fever. There was nothing to lose if it didn't work.

Lily felt a bit silly opening and closing the scissors over Lencha's listless form. Then, not knowing what else to do, she left the scissors open on the bedside table. Maybe in that position, the iron would draw out the fever. She could only hope.

Lily was eating breakfast when there was a knock on the door. It was Sal on his way to work. The man never seemed to have a day off.

"Just wanted to check on you. Everything all right?" he asked.

"I'm fine, but Lencha's not any better. I'm hoping her fever will turn soon."

"I can always drive to Chinatown and get the doctor."

Lily hoped it wouldn't come to that, but she nodded, grateful once again for Sal's kindness.

Sal pointed to a mound of greenery at the base of the steps. "I'm dropping off these plants too. They're from Catalina's garden. Betty says there's a lot of people in Palo Verde and Bishop who still need them."

Lily stared down at the aloe plants. Her eyes went blurry with tears. She wasn't used to such kindness.

Lily gave Sal a quick hug. "Thank you, thank you."

"It was nothing." He walked backward toward his truck, his cheeks flushing with embarrassment.

The aloe plants gave her morning purpose. The fog was thinning, and La Llorona had left them alone in the night. Their house was protected, and so was she, with the black stone hanging around her neck.

Lily changed into flannel trousers, an old blouse, and a heavy sweater and walked through the garden to the shed. Soon enough, people began to arrive with more stories about the weeping woman. They told Lily La Llorona had drifted through the streets of Palo Verde and Bishop, wailing and crying, "Cuidado, cuidado," until the wee hours of the morning.

People found her cries of warning as frightening as the phantom herself.

Everyone was scared of what she might do. Men were hesitant to go to work, worried they might be involved in an accident. Mothers were filled with anxiety at the thought of their children getting on the school bus. Women who worked in factories feared the machines might malfunction and cause serious injuries.

But the demands of their lives did not allow them to keep their children home or take days off. So with a sense of dread, they trudged to work and waved goodbye to their children boarding the bus, unsure if they would ever see them again.

Lily's visitors just wanted to share their fears with a sympathetic soul. They told their stories and left with grateful expressions, clutching their aloe plants, hope in their eyes.

After a busy morning, she took a short break for lunch, then returned to the shed. As soon as she entered, a hand shot past her, and the door slammed so hard, the rickety building shook.

Someone pushed her forcefully against the worktable.

It was Emiliano, his face inches from hers. He reeked of stale beer.

"Get away from me," Lily cried.

Desperation clawed at her chest, and she frantically fought to break free from Emiliano's grasp. She was trapped in a small space with a man whose eyes were filled with dark and menacing desire.

This was what Lily had always feared would happen. Why she'd left her childhood home. But moving away hadn't been enough to save her from Emiliano.

Her stepfather now stood between her and the worktable, blocking her access to the few things she could use as a weapon against him: the sharp point of a spade, a knife she used for cutting string. Panic set in. Lily was completely defenseless against him.

He lunged, grabbing the front of her shirt and ripping it open. She felt a tug at her neck and watched the necklace with the black stone fall to the ground. Emiliano fumbled with the belt on his pants. She felt dizzy. But if she fainted, Emiliano wouldn't care. He'd rape her while she was unconscious.

Lily roused herself enough to twist away from his grasping hands. He pushed his face into hers, and she managed to bite his jaw, blood blooming in her mouth.

A hand struck the side of her head. An explosion of dull pain brought a white flash to her eyes.

Lily staggered backward and cried out, as loudly as she could, "Help. Please. Someone, help!"

The door of the shed slowly opened, and beyond Emiliano, a figure stood in the middle of the yard.

It was a woman. Completely still. Staring.

Long dark hair. A somber gray dress. She looked like someone Lily had seen in old photographs. Like relatives from Mexico long ago.

Emiliano must have registered Lily's startled expression because he whirled around and, when he saw the woman, shouted, "Get the hell out of here. We're busy."

He slurred his words, spittle forming at the corners of his mouth.

The woman wasn't far away, but Lily still couldn't see her features clearly, and she wondered if the blow to her head had affected her eyesight.

If the stranger had heard Emiliano, she showed no sign of it.

He angrily seized Lily's arm and stamped his foot. "I said go!" he bellowed.

The woman in the gray dress vanished.

A blink of an eye later, she was standing right in front of them.

Lily could see her face now—her skin ashen, stretched tight against cheekbones as sharp as blades, lips black as ink and twisted into a menacing grin.

A death's head.

La Llorona.

Emiliano screamed.

Over the thumping of Lily's heart came a faint creaking. The woman's mouth was slowly opening, revealing rows of blackened teeth.

"Cuidado," she thundered in a voice so loud, Lily's bones rattled.

Emiliano dashed across the yard, his feet stumbling on the uneven ground. He headed for the gap in the back fence, but before he could reach it, La Llorona flew ahead of him, blocking his escape.

She became the same terrifying apparition Lily had encountered on the streetcar, draped in a wet white shroud.

Lily became aware of a new sound: the loud, cawing calls of crows circling above La Llorona.

Emiliano had fallen and was frantically trying to crawl away. La Llorona stood above him, claw-like hands on her hips, exuding anger and disgust. The veil covering her head did not obscure the strands of tangled hair and the fiery red eyes glaring down at him.

Lily's stepfather threw his hands over his face.

Something slithered out from beneath La Llorona's long and gauzy skirts: a snake the color of the earth, writhing and twisting, its body thick and sinuous, blending in with the ground beneath it.

La Llorona waved her hands. In a flash, the snake launched itself onto Emiliano's torso, slithering upward and sinking its fangs into his neck. Emiliano thrashed on the ground, hands clutching at the serpent, desperately trying to pry it off.

Only when La Llorona raised a skeletal arm high in the air did the snake stop its relentless attack. Like a dog recalled to its whistling owner, it disappeared under the white skirt.

Lily inched closer to Emiliano and gazed down at him. His neck and face were red and already starting to swell. He was still alive but barely.

When Lily glanced over at La Llorona, she was once again an ordinary woman dressed in somber gray. Lily could see her face now—not beautiful, but arresting, with large dark eyes, full lips, and a sad expression.

She had begged for help, and La Llorona had come to her rescue. To save her. Or to punish him.

La Llorona had shown a less frightening version of herself. The phantom Lily had long feared had come to her aid when she needed it most. But then Lily remembered her little brother Tomas, and something inside her snapped.

"Why?" she screamed. "Why did you take my brother?"

La Llorona shook her head, her lovely red lips pressed tightly together, for once silent.

La Llorona's face was wet with tears, but it was no normal flow. Tears fell like rain, soaking her dress.

"Didn't you do it?" Lily cried.

Still, the woman did not speak. She didn't need to.

The afternoon at Echo Park played out before Lily's eyes as clear as a movie. Tomas thrashed in the lake, frantically trying to stay afloat. But then he disappeared under the water and didn't resurface. He flailed deep in the murky water, panicked. There was no one pulling him down.

On the shore, his cousins screamed.

When the image faded, Lily knew the truth. Tomas had drowned. It had been just an accident.

A sliver of sun pierced the fog, gently warming Lily's head. La Llorona slowly turned and disappeared through the gap in the fence, like a neighbor departing.

When Lily turned back to Emiliano, he was dead. The crows which had earlier circled La Llorona now perched on the roof of the shed, watching Lily with gleaming eyes. The world around her seemed to shift. She didn't have to live in fear of this man anymore.

Lily left him where he lay. As if in a trance, she went straight to Lencha's room and discovered her aunt standing next to her bed, wearing a robe.

With a glint in her eyes, Lencha held up the scissors. "How did you know to leave them open like that?"

Lily shrugged. "I don't know. I just did." Her voice was hoarse, as if she hadn't spoken in weeks.

Lencha didn't smile exactly, but she was obviously pleased. "We'll make a bruja of you yet. You seemed to know exactly what to do."

Lily collapsed into a chair. "Emiliano's outside. Dead."

"The commotion woke me up." Lencha gave a nonchalant shrug. "I saw out the window. I didn't think you had it in you, summoning La Llorona like that."

Lily's mouth fell open. Lencha didn't seem fazed La Llorona had appeared in her backyard and a man was out there, dead by snakebite.

"I didn't summon her." Lily paused. "Or at least, I didn't mean to."

Lencha smirked. "Maybe not, but you're lucky she answered your call for help. It's a good thing she's been hanging around the neighborhood."

Lily bolted upright. "Do you think that's why she's been following me? That she somehow knew what was going to happen and she's been trying to warn me?"

"Who knows why she does what she does?" Lencha said. "But I know one thing. I need a bath."

Chapter 14

The day Emiliano died in Lencha's backyard was the last time anyone spotted La Llorona in Chavez Ravine. That afternoon, the fog cleared, and the sun shone down on the three hilly neighborhoods.

Lencha went back to her business in the shed. Throughout the ravine, the aloe plants tied with red string had dried up on the nails where they still hung. People were understandably hesitant to take them down too quickly.

Once again, the neighborhoods became lively places. Women hung wash on clotheslines, chatting together over fences. The joyful sounds of children echoed through the canyons. Men gathered together outside the markets, grabbing a smoke or a beer before heading home after a long day's work.

At Betty's insistence, Lily went to mass on Sunday at Palo Verde Church, sandwiched between Betty and Lencha on one side, and Sal and his girlfriend, Angie, on the other. Angie was a kind, big-boned woman who worked in a bakery at La Plaza in downtown Los Angeles.

After church, Angie invited everyone to her family's house in Palo Verde for menudo. Lily learned how Betty, Angie, and six other women planned to continue pushing for paved streets, sidewalks, and streetlights. Lily thought that was the sort of thing only college-educated people did and, after she'd had a glass or two of wine one evening, said as much to Betty.

"I may not have been to college, but I know what's right and what's wrong. And I've got a big mouth, and I'm not afraid to use it," Betty replied. "But you're young. You're smart. You should go to college."

"Me?" Lily echoed. The thought had never occurred to her.

"Who's stopping you?"

"For one thing, I need to work," Lily replied.

After her shifts at the factory and on her rare days off, Lily spent time with Lencha, learning more spells. While she found the spell work itself compelling, Lily thought it was a strange sort of business. The same people who begged for help one day often pretended not to notice her the next. Lily had found this behavior perplexing and mentioned it to Lencha.

"It's not you," Lencha had said. "People are funny about it sometimes."

"It" being brujeria.

Half the residents seemed to openly appreciate her aunt, while the other half treated her with suspicion. At least, until someone got sick, broke out in a strange rash, or had a streak of bad luck.

Lily looked forward to her lessons with Lencha. She learned the names of the herbs in the backyard, which ones helped to relieve gas, which to use for a toothache or to ease the pain of arthritis. Sometimes after work, Lily would stop at the botanica downtown and roam the aisles, looking for herbs grown in Mexico.

A few of the younger women in La Loma, intimidated by Lencha's stern demeanor, asked to see Lily privately. She listened to their worries: a boyfriend losing interest, a jealous woman making life miserable at work, a future mother-in-law trying to talk her son out of marriage. Lily would do the proper hechizos and was thrilled to learn they seemed to work.

Soon, many of the younger women in the neighborhoods would openly greet her in public, and if they didn't, Lily made a point to nod and smile. There was no reason for her to be embarrassed about her status as a bruja-in-training. She felt a sense of pride in her growing abilities, and she was enjoying helping others.

When Lily's mother invited her to move back home, Lily refused, saying her skills were needed in Chavez Ravine. She had visited her mother several times after Emiliano's death and was surprised her mother showed no curiosity about what had happened in Lencha's backyard.

Lencha said that's because her mother finally understood her new husband was a no-good cochino and was ashamed to admit it. Lily wasn't ready to forgive her mother yet for marrying that horrible man.

Lencha made no mention of Lily moving out, but when her aunt began to disappear some evenings without explanation, Lily guessed she was visiting her man friend. Eventually, when Lily pressed her about it, Lencha confessed this was the case.

To Lily's great surprise, the man was not only a gringo, but also a college professor of history. It was during one of those evenings Lily had a sudden realization: she needed to find a place of her own.

The very next day, Lily found a tiny one-bedroom cottage for rent around the block from Sal and Betty. With her salary and the extra money she was making from dispensing cures and spells, Lily could more than afford the payment.

The little house was rundown, with a rickety fence, but Lily didn't care. She only saw its potential. Lily scrubbed down every surface, made new curtains for all the windows using leftover material from work, and planted her own herb garden. Sal helped her turn the screened-in back porch into a workroom so the women who came to see her could enter through the backyard and avoid the prying eyes of nosy neighbors.

Sometimes, on a day off, Lily would explore the three villages of Chavez Ravine, wandering through the network of woods and gullies, walking up and down the steep hills and twisting roads. And she often spent time with Lencha, Betty, Sal, and Angie.

Whenever people gathered, eventually the conversation turned to La Llorona. It was strange, everyone agreed, the way she'd suddenly appeared, then vanished.

After a few weeks, Lily went to her first house party near the police academy—all the furniture moved into the backyard to make room for dancing. Betty was there, looking glamorous in bright red lipstick and dancing with her husband.

Lily stayed on the porch, too shy to dance with any of the young men who asked her. To her great surprise, Lencha arrived. Lily hardly recognized her aunt with her black dress and pinned-up hair.

Sal grinned, leaning against the porch railing opposite Lily, his arm around Angie.

Lencha joined them on the porch and accepted a glass of wine.

Soon, the porch's lumpy old couch and chairs were filled with women from the local citizen's group. Betty squeezed in next to Angie, a faraway look in her eyes.

The smiles had vanished from their faces.

When Lencha asked why they were so serious, Betty explained they had attended a city council meeting, where they discussed Chavez Ravine. They hadn't liked what they'd heard but decided to wait to tell everyone until they knew more.

"You can't keep bad news to yourself," Lencha said sternly.

Betty stared down at her hands.

"What did they say?" Lencha pressed.

Betty sighed heavily. "It was terrible. Some people called our neighborhoods blighted. Slums. They kept talking about a survey they did, saying a lot of the houses don't have toilets or running water."

"Substandard, they said," Angie grumbled. "Boy, did that make me mad. And then they had the nerve to talk about how we have nothing but dirt roads and no sidewalks, when the city hasn't done a single darn thing we've asked."

Chavez Ravine had some ramshackle properties, but there were plenty of nice houses too. Lily thought calling the area *blighted* was unfair, and she suddenly felt hot and prickly all over.

Sal was furious. He paced in the front yard, muttering.

Lily was only half listening to the conversation. Her thoughts had drifted back to La Llorona, the way she'd floated through the streets, wailing and shrieking, "Cuidado!" No one had known what she'd meant at the time, but now, Lily thought she understood.

When Lily glanced up, Lencha was staring at her with her with a slightly parted mouth. The look on her aunt's face told her they were both thinking the same thing.

"Is that why she was here, Tia? To warn us?"

That got everyone's attention.

Sal crouched next to Lencha. "Are you talking about La Llorona?"

Lencha didn't reply. Instead, she turned to Betty and Angie. "Those men you were talking about. They weren't just saying all that just to say it. What do they want to do?"

Betty and Angie exchanged glances. Lily's heart turned into a stone and sank. These were two smart, sensible women. Whatever they'd heard at that meeting was worse than they'd let on.

Betty cleared her throat. "They're talking about putting in a housing project."

Sal looked around wildly, like he expected one to sprout up in the street. "Here?"

"Yes, here." Betty's voice was sharp and tinged with anger. "We might have to move out." She paused, hands clenching into fists. "It was just a bunch of talk. Half of what they say at those meetings never happens, and a lot of us own our homes. We're American taxpayers. They can't just make us up and leave because they want to build apartments."

"They'll have to buy us out," Sal grumbled. "And you know what that means. They'll try to cheat us."

Lily noticed the panic in the faces of her new friends.

The news spread fast. The music stopped. So did the dancing. People went home with worry in their eyes.

Lily wondered what she would do if the city carried out its plans for Chavez Ravine. She was just a renter.

The man who owned her house, along with a half-dozen others, lived in Long Beach and only showed up to collect the rent from his tenants. He seemed like the kind of man who cared more about money than anything else, and if the city ever offered to buy his rundown properties, he would probably snatch up the cash without a second thought.

They walked toward La Loma in the cool night air, and Lily returned to the question haunting her.

"Do you think La Llorona was trying to warn us?"

Lencha shrugged. "If she knew something bad was going to happen, it would explain why she was here..."

Gooseflesh erupted on Lily's arms as she recalled the cries of the weeping woman. *Cuidado. Cuidado. Cuidado.*

To most people, La Llorona was a terrifying ghost. But to Lily, she was a protector. And a harbinger of something dark to come.

They entered La Loma with a rush of wind. From the distance came the lonely sound of a coyote howling.

Author's Note

If this is your first time reading one of my stories set in Chavez Ravine, a short explainer is in order.

First off, La Llorona, or the crying woman, is a legend from Latin American folklore who takes many forms. In some stories, she has cloven hooves, in others, she's a red-eyed skeleton. She sometimes wears black, sometimes white. In this story, La Llorona appeared in many ways, each inspired by the old tales.

Second, the neighborhoods of La Loma, Palo Verde, and Bishop are not the product of my imagination. They were once real, thriving communities where Dodger Stadium now stands.

The displacement of the residents, as foretold by the warning cries of La Llorona in this story, actually happened. The City of L.A. evicted the families in Chavez Ravine to make room for a public housing project, but that plan fell through for complicated political reasons.

Eventually, after the residents were given the boot, the city sold the land to Walter O'Malley, the owner of the Brooklyn Dodgers. The rest is history.

Two excellent books, *Stealing Home* by Eric Nusbaum and *Shameful Victory* by John Laslett, do a wonderful job explaining it all.

My mother and her family were among the evicted residents, and in some ways, they never got over it. These fictionalized Chavez Ravine stories are my way of keeping the memories of the neighborhoods alive.

Keep reading for a preview of:

A CHAVEZ RAVINE STORY

THE NIGHT LADY

DEBRA CASTANEDA

At night, danger lurks in the ravine.

Chapter 1

Los Angeles, July 1950

Jane Acevedo, on the lookout for the boogeyman, crept along the fence of her front yard, using the vines as cover. It was getting dark, and her mother had said she couldn't play with the other kids down the street. Not unless she wanted El Cucuy to snatch her away and drink her blood.

So far, all she'd seen with her pretend binoculars were her neighbors coming and going, but then she spotted Catalina Montez, the beautiful lady who lived down the road. Jane got to see her plenty at the empty lot across the street where Catalina grew plants for her cures. Her remedies were famous—even better than Vick's VapoRub.

Jane stood on an overturned washtub so she could get a better view. Blood dripped down Catalina's face. It made Jane feel all wobbly, but she couldn't stop watching, like a scary movie at The Brooklyn—she had to know what happened next. Besides, she'd been so bored having to stay in the front yard with nobody to talk to, and nothing much ever happened in Palo Verde.

And just like a movie, the door of the house next to the garden banged open, and Espy Gaten gave a dramatic cry, then ran down the steps. Espy, with her hair tied up in a scarf, didn't resemble a movie star like Catalina, but she was pretty too, just taller and skinnier. Espy helped Catalina into the house.

Jane would have loved to find out what was going on, but her mother didn't allow her to step foot past the gate. Not unless Jane wanted a swat on the *nalgas*. But Catalina with blood all over her face was even better than the gorilla girl matinee she'd seen. And besides, she was only going across the street. Jane checked for her mother to make sure she was still hanging laundry in the backyard, and she was.

Jane dashed across the dirt road and around the side of Espy's house, skirted the wild roses and thorns, then flattened herself against the fence so the *nopales* cactus wouldn't scratch her. Luckily, the kitchen window was open, and that's where the two women were, huddled together. She could hear Catalina crying, and when she managed a peek inside, standing on her tiptoes, she saw Catalina's torn dress, busted lip, and blood coming from an ugly cut above her eyebrow.

Jane couldn't picture Catalina getting into a fight like Uncle Beto. Maybe she'd fallen, or maybe someone got mad at her for one of her cures going wrong. But that was also hard to imagine—Catalina Montez was the most famous *curandera* around.

Keeping one eye on the front door of her house to make sure her mother didn't appear—in which case she planned to make straight for the back alley, jump a fence or two, and end up in her own backyard—Jane peered through the window again. Espy was walking back and forth in front of the stove as Catalina sat, looking as miserable as a kid on the first day of school.

"We should call the police," Espy said, in the same tone of voice Jane's mother used to threaten Uncle Beto.

"No, no, no," Catalina moaned.

The healer muttered something Jane couldn't hear, then the two women switched to Spanish, which Jane understood well enough to know they were having a secret conversation. Espy asked if Catalina couldn't hex the man who had done that to her, and Catalina said he deserved the worst magic she could summon, even if it meant she had to call on Santa Muerte herself. At this, Jane shivered because her mother would not even allow her to mention the saint of death with the face of a skeleton. But Jane's thoughts were spinning elsewhere.

Magic. *Magia.*

The two women talked about magic as if it were real, and Jane remembered something her mother had said about Catalina, that she wasn't just a healer but a *bruja*, a witch. Jane's father said there was no such thing, which had surprised Jane because if he believed in *El Cucuy* and *La Llorona*—and he did because he always said if Jane didn't behave, they'd get her—then how could he not believe in brujas?

"But we can't just let him get away with it," Espy said in a loud voice.

Catalina stood, slowly enough for Jane to hunker down so they wouldn't see her. "I'll figure out a way, Espy, and he'll be sorry he ever touched me. Can you help me home?"

"Why don't you stay here? You shouldn't be alone. Not after everything you've been through."

"I just want to take a bath. In my own place."

"Then I'll go with you," Espy said firmly.

A chair scraped against wood, and Jane knew it was time to get going. By the time the two ladies left the little house, Jane was standing on her own front porch. She watched them walk down the street.

When they disappeared from view, Jane put on her pretend binoculars, searching for the bad man who hurt Catalina.

More Books by Debra Castaneda

Dark Earth Rising
Themed novels that can be read in any order

The Root Witch
A beautiful forest. A terrifying legend. It's 1986. Two strangers, hundreds of miles apart, grapple with disturbing incidents in a one-of-a-kind quaking aspen forest.

The Devil's Shallows
Eight miles of mystery. One night of terror. Residents trapped in a remote neighborhood confront the unimaginable.

Circus at Devil's Landing
Creatures that howl in the night, a mysterious circus, and a clash between a ringmaster and a woman determined to rescue her captured lover.

The Copper Man
Haunted tunnels. Unexplained deaths. Eerie sightings. Decades after The Copper Man killed her brother, Leah Shaw returns to the remote mining town of Tribulation Gulch where a lethal mystery awaits.

A Dark and Rising Tide
When a massive storm surge hits the central coast of California, the ferocious surf destroys buildings, floods streets, and washes up something sinister from the depths of the Monterey Bay.

The Spore Queen
A charming reporter, an ailing tech mogul, and two strangers hiding secrets are brought together by a mysterious fungus, one that will either save them or destroy them.

Chavez Ravine Novels
Stand-alone novels set in Chavez Ravine, Los Angeles during turbulent times

The Monsters of Chavez Ravine
A 2021 International Latino Book Awards Gold Medal Winner! Before Dodger Stadium, dark forces terrorized Chavez Ravine.

The Night Lady
A rebel curandera, a plucky seamstress, and a young reporter are pulled into the investigation of a killer terrorizing Chavez Ravine.

The Haunting of Chavez Ravine
La Llorona is terrorizing people in the hills of Chavez Ravine, and a sassy curandera and her clever young niece must stop her.

The Christmas Cucuy
It's Christmas Eve, 1949, and Kiki's dreams are about to come true: she'll be singing at Palladium with her old bandmates. But when she threatens her rambunctious son with El Cucuy, her plans change.

ingramcontent.com/pod-product-compliance
ng Source LLC
rsburg PA
2011170626
300007B/2877